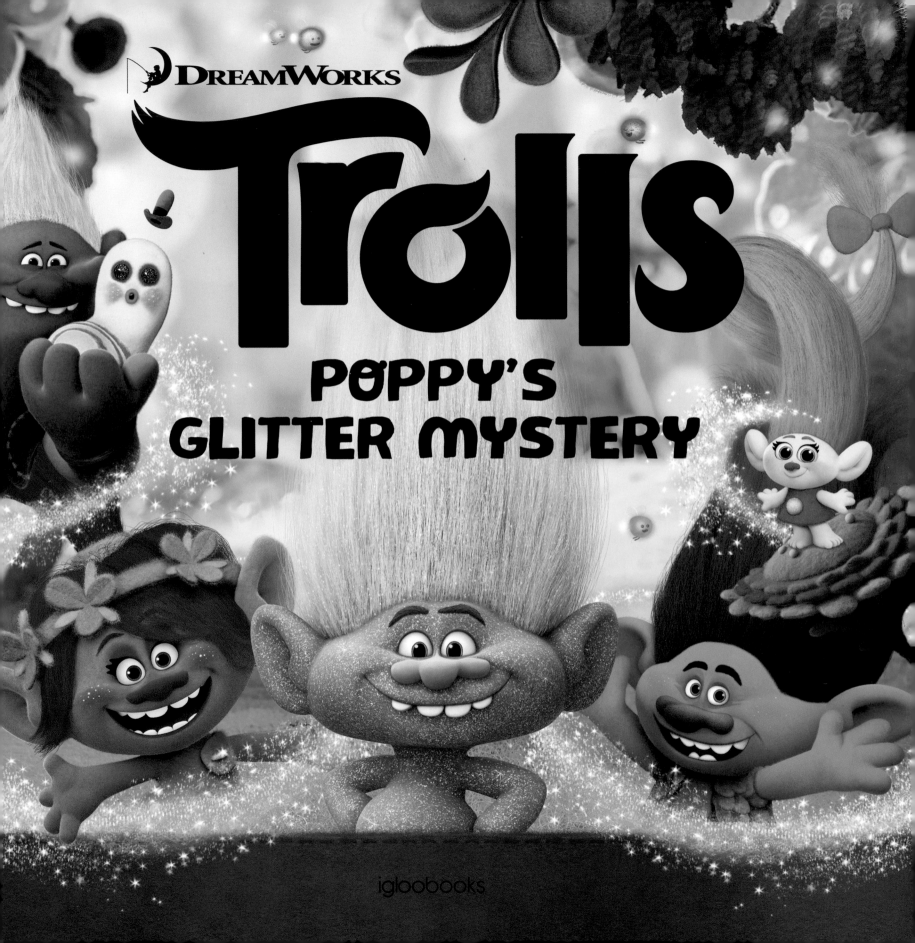

igloobooks

Published in 2017
by Igloo Books Ltd
Cottage Farm
Sywell
NN6 0BJ
www.igloobooks.com

Written by Rachel Chlebowski
Illustrated by Fabio Laguna and Character Building
Designed by Stephen Jorgensen
Edited by Gemma Rose

REX001 0717
2 4 6 8 10 9 7 5 3 1
ISBN 978-1-78557-747-5

Printed and manufactured in China

This Trolls book belongs to:

Sophie & Lauryn - from Nan Xmas 2017.

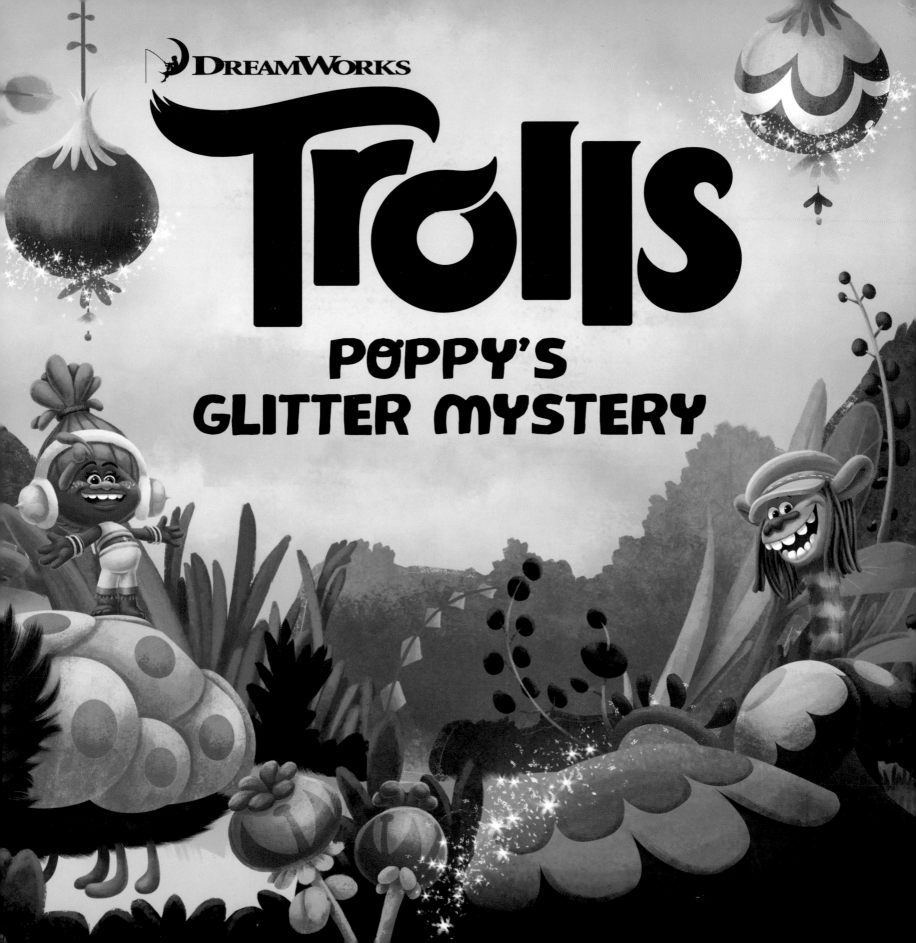

Meet the Trolls

POPPY

Meet Poppy, a relentlessly upbeat Troll who inherited her father's crown. Now queen of the Trolls, she loves to sing and knows everything sounds better with a cowbell. Poppy brings everyone together, Troll or otherwise.

BRANCH

Branch used to be a paranoid survivalist, who often wondered if he was the only sane one in town. He can still be grumpy sometimes, but Branch has now embraced his true colours and found his singing voice.

GUY DIAMOND

Our resident glitter Troll, Guy Diamond has heaps of body confidence and a unique idea of personal space. He is a party on two feet and his upbeat energy rubs off on whoever he's around.

SATIN & CHENILLE

Satin and Chenille are the trendiest Trolls in Troll Village. They were instrumental in putting together all of Poppy's outfits for her Coronation Celebration. These conjoined twins never wear the same thing twice.

SMIDGE

A teeny-tiny Troll with a shockingly deep baritone voice, Smidge enjoys weightlifting, listening to Swedish rock music and crocheting. She loves to squeeze in a quick workout during any dance number.

DJ SUKI

DJ Suki is the Trolls' resident DJ. Her DJ equipment consists of colourful critters, and she can always be counted on to lay down some beats for an impromptu musical moment.

COOPER

A rarity in Troll Village, Cooper is a fuzzy giraffe-like creature, with a playful grin plastered permanently on his face. He is always ready with a wicked harmonica solo and is full of enthusiasm.

FUZZBERT

The Troll that's entirely made of hair – only Fuzzbert's two feet are visible beneath a tuft of bright green Troll hair. He communicates using noises.

KING PEPPY

As the brave leader of the Trolls, King Peppy led his people to freedom from Bergen Town. 20 years later, he passed the Torch of Freedom to his daughter, Poppy.

BIGGIE & MR. DINKLES

Biggie is the biggest Troll with the biggest heart. He's a huge softie who never goes anywhere without his beloved pet worm, Mr. Dinkles.

Poppy was ready to try on a new dress that her fashionista friends, Satin and Chenille, had created for her. As queen of the Trolls, she never knew when she might be called on to go to an awesome party. However, when she walked into the dressing room, she saw that the dress was covered in glitter! Lots and lots of glitter.

"There's only one Troll who could have done this," Poppy said.

"Guy Diamond!" Satin and Chenille said at the same time.

"I'm going to find out what he's up to," Poppy said. "Luckily, Guy tends to leave a trail."

She followed his glitter footprints into the garden, but no Guy Diamond.

Next, she searched the cupcakery. Biggie was making fancy treats. Glitter sparkled here and there, but still no Guy Diamond.

Meanwhile, DJ Suki was mixing beats and making music with her Wooferbug.

"What is this tune missing?" she asked her Wooferbug.

"Glitter!" Guy Diamond sang, popping up out of nowhere.
With a poof, he covered everything in glitter.
"Yes! That's it," she said. Her new tune sparkled with light.
But Guy Diamond left as quickly as he had appeared.

DJ Suki was still jamming when Poppy arrived.

"I'm following the glitter to its source," Poppy said.

"Well, he went that way!" DJ Suki shouted over the music,
pointing in the direction that Guy Diamond had gone.

Then Poppy found Branch and Cooper.

"Guy glittered my harmonica,"
Cooper said. "Check this out."

Cooper let loose on his harmonica. The brightest notes ever
blew from it . . .

. . . and so did a lot of glitter, which landed right on Branch.

"I don't do glitter," Branch sighed, brushing off the sparkly dust.

"Well, come on, then," Poppy said, grabbing him by the arm.

"Let's find out what all this glittering is about."

Poppy and Branch searched Troll Village high and low.
Guy Diamond's trail of glitter was easy to follow, but
Guy was hard to find.

Poppy and Branch almost caught up with Guy Diamond at Maddy's hair salon. Everyone there was covered in glitter.

"I guess Guy was just here," Poppy said.

"Yep," said one Troll.

"Sure was," said another.

"But he didn't stay long."

The Trolls decided to join Poppy's search party. At the edge of Troll Village, the glitter trail led deep into the dark forest. The group of Trolls stopped, but Poppy took a deep breath and bravely pushed the leaves aside.

"Oh my gah!" exclaimed Smidge.

It was a giant **GLITTER PARTY!**

"Welcome to the biggest, brightest, most glittering party ever!" Guy Diamond cheered as his friends joined in with their newly glittering clothing, hair and accessories. "I'm so happy everyone could make it. Thank you for bringing the glitter," he added with a wink.

Biggie wanted to take a picture of the happy Trolls. On Poppy's count of three, they all said, **"GLITTER BURST!"**

The End